RICHARD ALI

TRANSLATED FROM THE LINGALA
BY BIENVENU AND SARA SENE

PHONEME
MEDIA

Phoneme Media
P.O. Box 411272
Los Angeles, CA 90041

ISBN: 978-1-944700-07-2

This book is distributed by Publishers Group West

Cover design and typesetting by Jaya Nicely

Printed in the United States of America

Phoneme Media is a nonprofit media company dedicated to promoting cross-cultural understanding, connecting people and ideas through translated books and films.

http://phonememedia.org

Mr. Fix-It

Editor's Note

Lingala, sometimes known as Ngala, is a Bantu language spoken as a first language by some five-and-a-half million inhabitants of the Democratic Republic of the Congo and the Republic of the Congo. An additional eight million people speak Lingala as a second language, as it serves as one of the region's most important lingua francas for commerce and culture. According to the constitution of the Democratic Republic of the Congo, it is officially a "statutory provincial language in northwestern regions," but because of the influence of the Congolese capital of Kinshasa, and, especially because of the great quantity of music written in the language—something Richard Ali A Mutu celebrates throughout *Mr. Fix-It*—it is widely considered to be the language of national identity.

A comparatively young Bantu language, Lingala emerged in the late nineteenth century, from the Bangi language used to facilitate trade along the portion of the Congo River leading to Kinshasa. Its use expanded once it was adopted by the King Leopold II of Belgium's Congo Free State as the means of communication for his merciless exploitation of the region for personal financial gain. Liberally absorptive and quickly evolving, Lingala has borrowed from many languages, both those native to the region and those introduced by its colonizers—in fact, the Lingala word for book, *bûku,* is borrowed from English and Dutch.

Contemporary Lingala-language literature has seen a recent uptick in both production and consumption, in no small part because of the work of *Mr. Fix-It* translators Bienvenu and Sara Sene, whose publishing house Éditions Mabiki published the original-language edition of *Mr. Fix-It*. It is significant to note that Richard Ali A Mutu's selection to the prestigious Africa39 list, which includes African and African diaspora writers like Chimamanda Ngozi Adichie and A. Igoni Barrett, makes him the only such writer to work primarily in an indigenous African language.

1

"...Write this down too: three bags of rice, four bags of beans, one restaurant-size pot, one brand new long-sleeved shirt—still in its packaging, one red tie for her father, one tie bar, one belt, a pair of sunglasses, one pair of shoes and a set of jewelry for her mother—don't forget the earrings, please!

"But..."

"But, but... What are you arguing for? Are we going to haggle over this? Is this the market?"

"No, but..."

"What do you mean, 'no but'? You have a problem with this? We aren't even finished yet. The girl's uncles haven't spoken, or her mom. Her older brothers and sisters have yet to state their demands..."

Ebamba's uncle sits there, speechless. The rest of his family and Ebamba himself are gesturing to him to just stop talking. There's no point. They'll just have to wait for the girl's family members to finish detailing their demands.

Ebamba's uncle can't help muttering to himself. *Alright, I'll stop talking. At any rate, what else could I say? I just can't stand what they are doing. Are they doing this on purpose or what? This just isn't right! Hell no!*

Just after Eyenga's dad stops talking, her mom immediately adds, "Thank you, my husband. As far as I'm concerned, I am not going to ask for much. Apart from what my husband has mentioned, I'll just add a stove and just three pairs of shoes… And, well, I'll stop at that!"

Then it is Eyenga's uncles' turn to speak. "We thank you, our brothers, for approaching us honorably through the main door of our compound instead of stealing in through the window. On behalf of all of Eyenga's uncles here, as well as those who got stuck in Kinshasa's traffic and those who've stayed behind in the village, we are content to ask you for these few items: two baskets of kola nuts, one bag of salt, one motorboat engine, four bicycles, five buckets of palm wine, and, finally, a small envelope for Uncle Antoine from the village, because he is very ill and we urgently have to buy some medication for him. We will just end here."

The sky has clouded over and the first raindrops are already beginning to fall, so the guests are quickly ushered into the house from the patio to continue the negotiations.

The rain suddenly comes crashing down, so the guests hurry into the house, but, small as it is, there is not enough room for everyone and Ebamba's friends have to find shelter inside the neighbors' house, while a third group rushes into the landlord's home.

"Uncle, we are very sorry, could you maybe just move over your chair a bit? You are sitting right beneath the crack in the roof, right where the rain seeps in the most."

"Sure, I can see some raindrops on my sleeve already."

"We are really sorry…"

"Not at all, it's like that in most houses in Kinshasa, these days…"

"What are you implying now, huh, uncle? What are you trying to say?"

Eyenga's father angrily jumps into the peaceful conversation between his wife and one of Ebamba's uncles. "Come on, Filipo!" soothes his wife "Why do always have to take things that way, huh? What did he say that was insulting in the first place? It is true, these days all houses in Kinshasa have leaking roofs…"

Now Eyenga's father gets really angry. "So, you find it normal to get this kind of remarks?"

"What kind of remarks? Did he say anything out of the ordinary?"

"How dare he talk like that? I will not allow anyone to make those kind of remarks about my house, ever!"

Eyenga's father is really furious now and starts yelling at his wife, while Ebamba's uncle keeps apologizing. "I didn't mean to be disrespectful, dear father-in-law. I have the same thing in my own home, you know. When it rains it leaks through the roof, and when it really pours down, the rain even sweeps in from beneath the door. I am really sorry. Don't be offended, please."

The rain keeps pouring down, stubbornly, and it is now seeping through the roof in more and more places. People are running out of dry places to sit. The rain is coming down as if someone had opened a giant faucet and the family is frantically putting out more and more buckets to protect the carpet. And then, as the living room is so small and people have to shift around to stay out of the rain, the decision is made to resume negotiations once the rain stops.

In the meantime, Eyenga has hid in her room. She is so ashamed she can't help crying. Her sisters and her mom follow her to soothe her. "Don't cry, sweet daughter, today we are all here to celebrate you…"

"Celebrate me, really? Or make me feel ashamed?"

"Ashamed of what?" cries out her mother, shocked.

"Look at the shameful things you are doing, all of you, mom! Do you really think this is normal?"

"What are we doing? I don't understand!"

"Mom, I'm sorry, just stop pretending you don't know what I am talking about. On the day dad's family came to see you to ask for your hand in marriage, did your family demand all that you are asking for now? What you are doing is really unbelievable! Are you giving me away in marriage or are you selling me at the market?"

"Are you dumb or what? Is that what you are crying about? Wait a minute, I'll be right back..." Eyenga's mother storms out of the room, leaving the girl to herself.

The rain keeps pouring down. It is getting really late. Forty-five minutes have already gone by. At this point, lights start to go out. There is a blackout in the city. Darkness is everywhere, in the house and in the whole neighborhood. The compound is completely inundated and water is streaming down the street, just like a river. The sewers start overflowing. And the rain keeps pouring down. A bad odor starts spreading through the house. Eyenga's family hastens to light up the petrol lamps. Everyone is pinching their nostrils shut. The strong smell of feces has really invaded the house now, but it is nothing new to Eyenga's family.

Eyenga's mother speaks up. "We apologize for this. Some bad neighbors on this street use every rainstorm as an opportunity to lift the tiles covering their toilets so they can flush them out… We have already complained again and again—we have even been to the town hall to complain. But the landlady of that place is the mayor's mistress. I tell you, this smell is caused by her cleaning out her compound's toilets…"

Ebamba's uncle asks, "Why don't you call in *Papa Molière*'s TV crew to report on this?"

"Ha! Forget about it, uncle! They have already spoken about it on TV, hadn't you heard? *Papa Molière* TV has already come over and they have shown her place on TV, but nothing's changed. I told you, the landlady is the mayor's mistress, nobody's going to bother her."

"This country is really going down the drain."

"Indeed it is."

7:30 in the evening. Time keeps ticking away. The rain will not relent, it is still pitch dark, mosquitoes are out in force too—and the bad smell is still strong. In the living room, the heat is unbearable. Ebamba takes off his jacket and tie, and he sits down next to his uncles. They are still waiting for the rain to subside, so that the roof will stop leaking. They have been given some beer, which they sip slowly, while they patiently wait for the rain to stop. The family has rolled up the curtains to let in some air.

The rain finally seems to subside, it's just dripping now. It will certainly clear up soon.

Eyenga's mother walks back into her daughter's room, accompanied by Eyenga's aunt. She asks her other daughters to leave, so they can speak in private, just her, her elder sister, and Eyenga. "Well, Eyenga, my daughter, it is no longer raining, so we can go back into the living room and wrap up our negotiations, but first I would like you to listen to what your aunt Batondo has to say."

Aunt Batondo speaks up. "My daughter, you may have grown, but you are still a child in our eyes. Your mother, my younger sister Bongesa, has told me that you are crying and fussing too much over the way things are going today... It's quite natural, and I understand, but you must know that between two people, when it really comes down to marriage, that is when families are officially invested in a relationship, it is no longer just something between a man and a woman, but a matter involving both families—and therefore lots of different people: the parents, the uncles, and so on. All of those people have rights according to our customs. They are entitled to asking for different gifts so they can allow you to go in peace and with their blessing into the arms of your husband and his family."

Eyenga replies, "I am not saying that's not true, aunt, but tell me, do people usually ask for all the things mom, dad, and my uncles are asking for? Don't you think we are embarrassing ourselves? What if they cannot afford to give all that you are demanding to have? Hasn't it crossed your mind that if that happens I will remain under your roof for even longer? I am the eldest and you have been supporting me for nearly thirty years!"

"Don't worry, my child. They are still going to discuss the terms of the deal. Besides, bear in mind that if that guy really loves you, he's going to do his damnedest to bring in all we have asked for. So, it is actually just a way for us to find out if he can really support you and whether he really loves you."

"Your aunt is right," adds Eyenga's mother, "and besides things are very different these days from when I was young. Back then, it is true that they only asked for salt and some kola nut. It was the good old days when we still lived according to the traditions of old. Now things have changed. When you have a daughter, you have a readymade treasure, as they say. Just think of what we have been through to support you, paying for your studies, paying for your food, for your clothes, for the doctor when you were ill, the money to make you pretty, and so on. And now you want to walk out on us. Don't you think it is a nice opportunity for us to get some of that money back? When you are settled in your household, it's not like we can come bother your husband all the time!"

"But, mom!"

"Again? That's enough! They are calling us, don't you hear? Clean up your face, dry your tears, put on some perfume, and let's go, quick!"

II

The rain has stopped. The power is back on. The bad smell is gone. A soft cool breeze is sweeping into the house. But it really is impossible now to sit outside; the whole yard is flooded over. The water is slowly draining, but it will take buckets and sweeping to get rid of it. And the neighbors are coming in to help, with pails and squeegees.

The street is flooded too. It has only been two months since the Chinese finished paving it and building the sewers, but the sewers are already beginning to get blocked up by all the trash the locals are throwing out: plastic bottles, all sorts of bags, leaves, and assorted garbage.

Some people said that the Chinese had not done their job properly. The road already had potholes here and there. Others said it was the handiwork of the neighborhood's witches, and in particular the witches on that street, who were opposed to the President's *"5 chantiers"* for the country's development. Those witches claimed nobody had asked for their permission before getting started with the construction, and they hadn't received their due, so the ancestors, who own the land, couldn't approve. So the road is certainly going to get worn out very fast, if nobody comes around to pay what is due. That's what they promised, just like in that story by Sene Mongaba "Bokobandela."

The locals were more and more afraid of the curse: just in the past month there had been six accidents, and even last week a little child was run over as he was crossing the street near the Shell gas station. He died instantly.

That sad matter had been brought before the mayor, who, as usual, laughed it off and simply promised to come and visit the good citizens of the street. The locals were still waiting for him to make good on his promise, but that's another story for some other time.

So, the rain was indeed over.

In the living room the negotiations had picked up again.

"Thank you, Father, for allowing me to speak. I am young Ebamba's uncle. I have brought him up and taken care of him since he was a little boy. As you probably all know, he lost both his father and mother when he was only twelve. Your daughter here, for whom we have come to pick up the dowry list today, must have told you already..."

Eyenga's mother looks pained. "No, Father, she didn't tell us. That's so sad. We really didn't know..."

"No harm done, ma'am. Now you know: his parents both died on the same day, in the most awful way. They were onboard a plane, and the pilot lost control of the plane during landing, and there was a crash... Nobody survived. We had to mourn them without having their bodies to bury, and their remains have never been found. The worst part is that the same airline had at least ten similar accidents during that same year, but they were never bothered by the authorities, and to this day we have only received a small amount of what the insurance was ordered to pay us... We are even tired of insisting on being paid our due. Apparently, the airline is owned by a minister, some even say the owner is a relative of the President."

"Oh my, this country!" Eyanga's father laments.

"Indeed, Father, if I go on telling you about it, I could go on all night... It is a shameful, sad, and complicated case. I could go on for hours, but, well, this won't be the last time we meet. We are family now, so we will definitely see each other often, and you'll certainly get a chance to hear the full story some other time. I've already told you what matters. Ebamba is an orphan, but that is not why we have gathered here. He's all grown up now. He's already a strong young man and he's the reason we are here today to discuss his tying the knot with your daughter Eyenga. So let's get back to our discussion."

A long silence followed his words. All faces had lost any trace of joy and some looked angry at the thought of the scam the insurance was putting them through, but, as Ebamba's uncle had said, they were around that table to negotiate a couple's union. Ebamba's uncle called over his friend who was in charge of taking notes of all that was being said and went on, "Father, we have listened with great attention to all you have said and we have written down everything. Just to be sure, let me ask my friend, Uncle Engulu, to re-read all that you are asking for."

Ebamba's adoptive father, Uncle Ebende, sat back down, while the bystanders clapped hands at his words. Uncle Engulu stood up, holding a sheet of paper and a pen, and spoke up. "Thank you so much, dear older brother Ebende, for giving me the floor. Let me then repeat the list of all that the bride's family is asking for."

He cleared his throat, adjusted his reading glasses, and, carefully holding his paper, he looked around at his audience once more and said, "Two goats, one male and one female; twenty kegs of palm wine; a bag of salt; a sofa and set of chairs; a plasma TV; a cable box; an iron; a washing machine; two three-piece Versace suits for her father; two pairs of shoes, one black and one brown, size 45; two top quality bottles of perfume; 12 yards of superwax fabric for her mother; three bags of rice and four bags of beans; one industrial-size cooking pot; one brand new long-sleeved shirt, still sealed in its wrapping; one red tie; one tie bar; one belt; a pair of sunglasses; one pair of shoes and a set of jewels and earrings; one stove; three pairs of flat shoes for her mother; two baskets of kola nut; one more bag of salt; a motorboat engine; four bicycles; five buckets of palm wine; one small envelope of money to buy medication; and finally, $2,500. And that's it!"

The whole audience hangs on to those final words. It's as if they are holding their breath. They don't even look at each other.

So, uncle Engulu hastens to add, "This paper lists all that you have asked for and we have faithfully noted. I give you back the floor."

Uncle Ebende stands up and while uncle Engulu sits down, claps his hands to signal he is ready to make his final remarks. "Thank you very much, Engulu. I believe all of us have heard what you said. Is there anything missing from that list? If you think we have omitted something, please let us know now and we will add it."

As everyone kept silent, he then added, "That's enough, then, I think. We have listened to your demands.

Soon we will return to offer what we are going to give you."

III

Knock knock knock!
Bang bang bang!

Inside, nobody stirs.

Knock knock knock!
Bang bang bang!

"Who is it?"

No one replies, but the knocking on the door resumes.

Knock knock knock!

"Who's there?!"
"Open the door! And don't keep me waiting!"

"Who are you? What do you want? Stop banging on that door!"

"Hey, Ebamba, don't play with me! Hurry up, open the door!"

Ebamba rushes out of bed, his heart beating madly. He suddenly recognizes the voice of Mama Mongala, his landlady. He stands up, puts on his shirt without even taking the time to check himself in the mirror, and opens the door.

At first he only opens the door a crack to look outside. He then peeks out to see if it's really Mama Mongala, his landlady. The sizzling hot sunlight blinds him and he can't see right away. He squints and opens his eyes as wide as he can. He sees that it is indeed his landlady, Mama Mongala, but she has turned her back to the door and can't see him. Ebamba stares at her. He really is astonished that she has come to knock on his door so early in the morning. His head starts spinning from thinking and he tells himself that it's not the first time she has come to see him, after all, difficult and hard as she is. Fine then, he is going to find out what it is all about.

He opens the door wide, draws open the curtains and calls out to his landlady, "Mama Mongala, good morning!"

Mama Mongala turns around to face him, looks right at him, and sucks her teeth aggressively. "Oh, go to hell! Good morning, alright! Today is the day you get out of my house!"

Ebamba is taken aback. "Why? What is the matter?"

"You are surprised? You haven't seen anything yet! I'll show you surprised, boy!" Then, less loudly, she adds, "This world is funny! You would think that people just don't like to receive acts of kindness!"

"What have I possibly done, Mama Mongala? What is so awful that you can't even wait to sit down and explain it calmly? It's still early morning, on a Sunday. Can't we just sit down and talk about it? So that you can tell me what the unforgivable thing I have done is for you to kick me out of your house, all of a sudden, with no notice?"

"No notice, you say? You want to intimidate me with your laws and regulations, in my own house?"

"No, that's not what I meant. I just wanted to say that we could peacefully address the situation…"

She has been talking so loudly that all her other tenants have woken up and gathered to see what is going on. Mama Mongala is not the kind of person who can talk softly. Whatever the matter at hand, she speaks with a booming voice. Hearing all the commotion, the dogs in the courtyard start barking along and everyone is buzzing with surprise. What can possibly be the problem?

There are these kinds of days, when the will to live just escapes you. You find yourself wondering what you could possibly have done wrong on this Earth. Why bad things always befall you. The answer is simply that you are a human and this is the lot of humans in this world.

The six o'clock sun is shining as brightly as if it were already noon. A slight breeze softens it. Yesterday's rain was really something.

On Ebamba's street, three houses had been completely flooded, and a roof had been blown off another. In other compounds several trees had lost their branches. Yes, the downpour had been truly terrible, and Mama Mongala's compound hadn't been spared either. She had been pained to discover that her beloved avocado tree had been thrown to the ground.

On the next street over, the wind had blown down walls. A pair of twin infants had died. Their mom had lit a petrol lamp because the power was out. Sadly, she had neglected to blow it out before going to bed and the kids had burned to death. In the morning, that version of events left people unconvinced. How was it possible that only the kids had died and the parents had been spared? Other even added that the house had plainly not burned, and that even though the kids had burned to a crisp, the bed they were sleeping on had been left intact. That definitely looked like an act of dark forces. Things don't happen that way. It was clear that things never happened that way. People were really in an uproar that morning because of it, and some had even gone to confront the twins's father about it. They had come with sticks, spears, machetes, and several other makeshift weapons to kill him, as it was clear to them he had brought about his kids's death with his sorcery.

Sunday is the day that business is taken care of. As the poet says, fair weather returns after rain. What is amazing, though, is that in this city that's not the way things go. The rain always leaves disaster in its wake. Here you have a flooded house, there someone was shocked to death, on the next street a tree was felled, or its branches fell off, the ground caved in, roofs were blown off, people are left homeless or trapped and have to be helped out of their homes. Others hid in their homes to protect themselves from the sewer's stench and so on.

Since people are now used to the situation, this state of things has become the new normal. But this is certainly not normal. As some newspeople shout: *Eza normal te!* It's not right!

The sun shines warmer, the sky is clear again. The rain has cleared all the previous night's clouds. But it's the kind of heat that brings back the rain. Now, during the rainy season, the rain pours down for two or three days in a row. On the news, some people like to play the scaremongering game, they claim that it's a sure sign that the end of the world is approaching. To them, Armageddon will take place right at the end of the rainy season. The public's fears grow every day: what is going to happen? Will it all come to an end?

That morning, the sun is already scorching the earth. It's seven o'clock. In the compound, Mama Mongala has stopped shouting, but she still looks furious. Ebamba drags out two chairs and offers a seat to Mama Mongala so they can talk things through, but she angrily refuses.

"I'm not going to sit down!" The chair remains empty, she stands there, arms crossed. Ebamba sits down in silence. Mama Mongala barks down at him. "You think you can treat me like a fool, Ebamba, don't you?" Wagging her finger at him, she goes on, "You think you can play with me? Answer me!"

Softly, like someone who's weary of loud noises, Ebamba replies, "What have I done to you?"

"What have you done? What have you done, is that what you are asking me?"

"For God's sake, Mama, yes—what have I done to you?"

"So, you pretend you don't know! You don't know what you have done, you say. Where were you last night and what time did you get back?"

Ebamba looks puzzled, he's now truly surprised. What's the matter? He opens his mouth to speak. "So, is this the only reason you got me out of bed at the break of dawn to shout at me?"

Mama Mongala shoots back, "Does it surprise you?"

"Why wouldn't I be surprised?"

Mama Mongala moves closer toward Ebamba, who is still rooted to his chair. She loosens the knot in the fabric wrapped around her left hip, shakes the cloth a bit, and makes a tighter knot. Hands on her hips, she takes a deep breath and snorts. Twisting her mouth, she says, "Ebamba, I asked you a question. Where were you last night?"

"I went to meet my girlfriend's family to ask for the dowry list, so we can get married."

"Huh. And you say it with no shame, you are planning to marry."

"What, why would it be a problem? Why should I be ashamed of getting married? Do I need to ask you if I can get married? Are you joking?"

"Let me ask you, when you moved in, didn't you see that there are plenty of girls in this compound already?"

"Of course, I saw them alright…"

"So then, how did it get into your head to go chase girls elsewhere?"

"Mama Mongala, I really don't understand what you are getting at. I came here to rent an apartment, not to date girls from the compound. When I moved in, I was already dating my present girlfriend. What was I supposed to do?"

"You already had a girlfriend? Do you know how many people I turned down as tenants before you came along? Do you know why I took you in? Look, I am going to be clear with you. My daughter Maguy is waiting for you. You are going to marry her, or I'll kick you out of the compound!"

"What are you talking about? When I moved in here, did we sign a paper saying I would marry her?"

"Well, we are signing it now. I'm telling you, from this moment on, Maguy is your wife! I don't even want to see your girlfriend's shadow around here or you'll see what I am capable of."

"God almighty!"

Ebamba's mouth is wide open with amazement. He is petrified. Mama Mongala turns around to leave, then thinks better of it and walks back up to him. "Now that you know, be careful what you do. I'm dead serious. If you try to deceive me, you'll see." Having said that, she turns her back to him and leaves, leaving Ebamba there. Ebamba remains in his chair, frightened and sad. His problems are crushing him. What is he going to do? What has he done wrong? What is going to happen to him? Where can he possibly go? He is already two months late on his rent. Same thing for his electricity and water bills. Until today, it hadn't occurred to him that his landlady hadn't chased after him to get her rent money.

Some days, when he comes home from making the little hand-to-mouth deals he comes up with to survive, tired and broke as he is, Maguy, the landlady's daughter, brings him nicely cooked meals. Sometimes she even gives him money or hands him enough for a drink, or brings over some other small gift. Now it dawns on him that those were all signs that he was supposed to date and marry her.

His head feels impossibly heavy from everything he's just learned, so he just sits there, a hand to his cheek. *Good God, how am I going to get out of all this? I love Eyenga, and her family expects me to give her a long list of things and a huge amount of cash before I marry her. I don't even know where to start to put together all they are asking for. And now my landlady jumps in with this matter of her daughter. How am I going to unravel all this? Maguy is a pretty girl alright, but I can't cheat on the woman I love and I've just promised to marry. God knows I'm not that young any more and I need to find a woman and start a family. I'm thirty-eight already. And I have no children, no good job. My life is really a failure. How am I going to end up?*

He is overwhelmed with all the questions and doubts whirling around in his mind. His head in his hands, he can't hold back the tears. He's done for. Images from his life start parading in his mind. How he blew his chances at a good job three times.

Ebamba had a friend from a wealthy family. His friend's father was a manager at a public service. One day, once Ebamba had graduated from college, his friend told him that at the bank where he worked they were hiring new graduates. It would be a great opportunity for Ebamba and his friend encouraged him to rush there with his resume and apply for the job.

His application was promising: he had a great grade point average and had even graduated with honors. He had an excellent command of foreign languages, like English and French. He was good at operating computer programs. So the bank manager let him know that he was quite favorably impressed with his resume and invited him, along with several other candidates, to sit for a written test.

He passed the test with flying colors and received an invitation for an interview, where he would take an oral test in English and French. He did well on that test too, and he was told he had passed. So his name, as well as the names of the other applicants who had passed that test, were sent on to one of the directors of the bank. The director sent an invitation to each of the successful candidates to interview on different dates. On the day of Ebamba's interview, the director had him come into his office and after closing the door behind him, started asking him questions. Ebamba was dressed like a prince for the occasion. A stylish tie around his neck, a shiny suit, chic cologne. He racked his brain to come up with his most refined English and French to impress the director.

The director was pleased with Ebamba's efforts and expressed his satisfaction. He was a foreigner. He had Asian traits, but the complexion of a white man. He was wearing a short-sleeved shirt with a fat red tie, and he had a slightly round belly. He was short and his red lips looked a bit like a woman's. The director was wearing tiny round glasses and his hair was curly and rather long, shiny with some product. His arms looked very hairy. He rocked back and forth on his chair, smiling as if he were really happy with Ebamba's performance, then he stood up, opened a drawer, and fished out Ebamba's file.

"Young man, I am really impressed. You are very bright."

Ebamba's eyes opened wide, happiness welling up in him. But the director was not yet done.

"However, I must tell you that we don't hire people this easily here..."

Ebamba's smile froze on his face and he frowned slightly. He suddenly remembered that his friend Matuka had told him a very strange story he had refused to believe. He wondered for a moment whether the same thing was not going to happen to him.

His childhood friend Patrick Matuka had been his schoolmate for years, and they had even graduated together. One day, he told Ebamba a horrible story. He was about to be hired by one of the most important companies in the country, but he was told that before the hiring decision could be made final he would have to produce a sample of his sperm in a small plastic cup that he was handed on the spot, and which he would then have to hand over to the manager of the company. He was so frightened by the odd request that he left the premises and never went back.

Ebamba wondered in his heart, *Good God, is this what's going to happen to me too?* He started shaking a little, but he told himself to stop worrying, he wouldn't come to any harm, his lucky star would protect him. He didn't move, he swallowed hard, and a heavy drop of sweat slid down his back.

"You know, you are a handsome young man, *Eeebamba*!" Ebamba shook his head lightly and made a half-smile as if to thank him for the compliment and the director went on. "Look, I can have you hired at the bank today. You'll start making a lot of money and you'll get to go on business trips. You are a sharp, handsome young man..."

Ebamba relaxed and smiled, as he started breathing freely again. He stopped perspiring and he found he could swallow normally again.

The director stopped nodding, stared at Ebamba's smile and abruptly added, "Listen, if you want all of this, you can have it on just one condition. If you sleep with me today, you can start working here tomorrow."

Bam! A thunderbolt shot through his heart. The young man opened his eyes and his mouth equally wide. A horrible, shameful sound had just entered his ears. He was left speechless. He felt like an electric shock had gone through his body. He felt frightened and dirty as if he had already accepted the director's sexual advances.

The director just stood there, looking hard at Ebamba and waiting for his answer. Finding nothing to say, Ebamba just lowered his head. The director looked at him and added, "What, are you scared? Have you never done it before? It's not going to last for long and it's not going to hurt. It will just feel good."

He got closer to Ebamba to touch him and start caressing him. Ebamba got up abruptly and pushed the white guy's hand away with some force. Startled and somewhat fearful, the white guy quickly took a step back.

Ebamba walked to the door and as he was about to step out, the white guy told him, "Look, if you change your mind, don't be afraid to come back, I'll wait for you." Ebamba sucked his teeth loudly and stormed out, banging the door behind him.

A cool breeze is blowing, the sky is darkening. The sun is setting near the Congo River, round like a ball of fire, red as blood. The surface of the river is untroubled. The wind is getting colder and passersby shiver. Night sets in, the sun vanishes from the horizon. In the sky, several types of birds are noisily rushing back to their nests, while the trees are slowly swinging their branches in the breeze. The wind is humming a song as if to say it is going to rain soon…

It's Saturday, the day when Kinshasa is at its most hectic. Kinshasa full of joy, Kinshasa home to life and its troubles. Kinshasa home to beer of all kinds: Nkoy, Moprima, Turbo, Skol… Kinshasa, the land of bursting joy in all its forms… It's true, you may live to be one hundred years old, but if you have never seen Kinshasa, you cannot say that you have truly lived. You have to see Kinshasa at least once, you have to see the Congo River.

We're approaching 6:12 in the evening. The bars are already crowded. In Niangwe, in Kimbondo, in Tshibangu, in Super, in Beau Marché, at Muguylaguyla and, topping it all, in Matongé Oshwe, the party is in full swing. Goat and chicken is roasted and eaten as enthusiastically as candy, drink is overflowing. Dance is everywhere. Kinshasa is the land of music, the land of *ndombolo*.

We're approaching 9:05 in the evening. The snake-girls are beginning to come out. You look at them, their beauty will bring tears to your eyes. They shine like gold. Some wear miniskirts, others just leggings, some wear superwax wraps, others skin-tight pants. They roam everywhere, looking for someone to bite, or someone who'll take a bite at them. You can find them along Avenue du Stade, around Inzia, at Yolo Nord, at Boulevard… The nameless girls, the givers of joy, the horse-girls whom anyone can ride. The girls from Bongolo… They come in all shades of color: black, chocolate brown, white, mixed, albinos... In all sizes: short, tall, medium-height, dwarves... And some are mute, disabled...

At a bar called Muguylaguyla, Ebamba and his friends are dancing to the notes of Ya Jossart: as they say, walk on the turtle's back, and then swell your chest. They dance Mama Siska... Beer has taken hold of them, they are getting drunk and they are starting to do things they can't really control. Ebamba finds himself feeling up his friend's girlfriend, who slaps him and brings him back to reality. Thankfully, he then snaps back to a normal human state right away.

Ebamba's girlfriend, Eyenga, had also come along, but she had already left because she wasn't feeling well. Ebamba had walked her to her house and then, since it was his old friend's birthday party, had gone back to join his friends who were dancing and drinking at the Muguylaguyla.

The party goes on and on, and it gets better and better. The rain has disappeared, carried off by the wind, leaving behind a cool breeze. You dance and dance and you don't even break a sweat. The few raindrops have only boosted everyone to keep the party going and people are dancing away and having fun.

It's 1:05 in the morning.

Knock knock…

Knock knock…

Ebamba is standing at the door to his compound, the gate is already locked for the night. He knocks in hopes that someone will hear him and let him in. He can't even call some neighbor to open the door because his cell-phone is missing. He has lost it at the party, dropped it from his pocket while he was dancing. Its new owner had picked it up and hurried away with it.

No one is coming. He is beginning to lose patience, but the beer is taking its toll on him and he just doesn't have the strength to climb over the wall. He just wants to crawl into his bed and sleep. Discouraged, he sits down, his back to the wall…

1:30…

He hears someone's steps approach, someone's opening the door. The gate squeaks open, he stands up to let himself in. His eyes focus on the person standing there. It's Maguy. She's just wearing a revealing wrap, barely covering her chest.

As they politely exchange a greeting, Maguy can smell the scent of beer all over Ebamba, as he walks past her toward his apartment.

It's pitch dark in the compound. Everyone's sleeping soundly. That night, they had forgotten to unleash the dogs in the yard, so the silence is complete. No one stirs.

Ebamba skulks to his door, gets out his keys, and lets himself in.

Maguy stays behind to lock the gate and then rushes back to her home.

It's 1:40… A cool, smooth hand is caressing Ebamba's penis. Ebamba feels his pleasure rise. Those same hands then unbutton his shirt and go on to play with the hair on his chest. A wave of desire and pleasure engulfs Ebamba.

The hands pursue their work. Ebamba, still shrouded in sleep, feels as if he's going to die. He feels the touch of a pair of juicy lips sucking the skin on his chest, biting him lovingly. His body starts burning up. All the hair on his body stands up. It feels so delicious he has goosebumps all over.

Desire wins over sleep. He begins to realize that this is definitely not a dream. He opens his eyes and he is truly startled to see a woman there.

"What?" he begins. Maguy lets go of his body and takes a step back. Ebamba comes back to his senses and is taken aback with what is going on. "What the hell is this? How did you get in?"

"What are you afraid of?" Maguy asks, so sweet that any ordinary man would just surrender, no questions asked. "What is so worrying, huh? Am I killing you, am I hurting you? You left your door open and I have come in to make you feel good…"

"Make me feel good?!"

"Hush, stop talking," Maguy says, untying her wrap.

To Ebamba's eyes, Maguy looks just like Eve in the Garden of Eden—her soft, brown body, with its round, firm breasts, standing there, her gaze fixed upon him.

Maguy draws closer to Ebamba, who's already trapped in her net. He is mute, his body shakes a little. He opens his mouth, but nothing comes out. Maguy takes off his shirt and kisses his lips.

Maguy slips down Ebamba's pants and she takes them off him completely. He just lets her. Then they fall back together on Ebamba's bed. The bed squeaks beneath them. The effect of the booze has completely worn off, now. Ebamba starts sweating everywhere, as their naked bodies come together.

There is no going back. Ebamba feels like he's going crazy, bloodshot eyes and all. He surrenders, he gives his everything, he lets Maguy play with him in any way she wants. The girl does to him all that she can think of. Everything spins around him, he's losing his mind completely. Never seen anything like that.

"It will be a grenadine and soda for me, please."

"Oh come on, you have really stopped drinking?"

"I told you, Tshiamwa, I don't want to touch a drop of beer again."

"Haha—be serious, that's a drunkard's promise!"

The waitress is standing there, waiting for Tshiamwa to say what he's going to have. "Mama, bring me a cold Primus." The waitress jots down their order and leaves. "Now, pal, tell me everything from the beginning. How has it come to this? I really don't understand."

"Ah, Tshiamwa, don't push me. It's not easy..." Ebamba lowers his head and buries his face in his hands. They are facing each other, he and his friend Tshiamwa, the table between them.

At this time of the day, the bar isn't crowded yet. It's just 12:30. The sun is shining so bright it burns your skin, but it's cooler in the bar. They are sitting under a great *lid-ame* tree, at the bar named *Sous le Madamier, Chez Pasteur,* in Bandal.

After a few moments, Ebamba lifts his eyes, shakes his head and, looking at his friend Tshiamwa, sighs. "Pal, I don't even know where to start."

"Well, isn't it why you invited me here? You don't want to talk about it, after all? What are we going to talk about then?"

"No, no, I'm going to get to it... But it's not easy, pal..."

"Ebamba!"

Ebamba lifts his gaze and eyes his friend again. The waitress is back with the drinks. She puts the bottles and their glasses down on their table. Their drinks look really well chilled.

"Thank you!"

The waitress leaves them and sits back down at a discreet distance.

Tshiamwa takes his beer and pours it. They clink their glasses, make a quick toast, and drink up. Ebamba puts down his glass, licks his lips, and takes a deep breath. Tshiamwa pours some more beer into his own, with the deep satisfaction of quenched thirst.

"You remember the daughter of my landlady, Mama Mongala?"

Tshiamwa jolts up in surprise—Ebamba's words have caught him in an unsuspecting moment, as he was busy nursing his glass. He gives a puzzled reply. “Sure! Of course I remember her! Maguy, is it?”

“Right! Her.”

“What’s she done? Is that what this is all about?”

“Yes, it’s her, pal. That girl and her mother have tricked me.”

A bit lost, Tshiamwa interrupts Ebamba. “Wait a minute, pal, Maguy and her mom—what have they done to you exactly?”

Ebamba looks his friend in the eye and says, “Tshims, Maguy is pregnant with my child.”

“What? Are you kidding?” Tshiamwa can’t hide his surprise, his mouth is wide open. “How did it happen?? And what about Eyenga then?”

“Well, that’s why I asked to see you, man, so we can talk things over. I don’t know what to do. I’m screwed.”

“What I don’t understand is, how did you get that far? What brought this about? Correct me if I’m wrong, they can’t have forced you, right?”

“No, man, no… Well, to be honest, if I should look at how it all happened, well, you could say I’ve been forced, yes…”

“Huh!” Tshiamwa just can’t believe it and with a mocking smile insists, “Tell me the truth, how did it come to pass?”

“Pal, do you remember the day of Matuka’s party, at Muguylaguyla?”

"His birthday? Of course, I remember… You were shitfaced, by the way."

"Right, that night. Well, when I got back home that night, pal, you know…" Ebamba tells his friend the whole story, from A to Z. He describes everything down to the last detail. Tshiamwa listens attentively, with the respect of a good friend, but he can't help making surprised noises while Ebamba tells the story.

"Pal, how far along is she now?"

"Just a month!"

Tshims shakes his head, scratches the stubble on his chin. "What's the plan now, you think? She gets an abortion, right?"

"No, man, what are you talking about!" Ebamba's heated reaction leaves no room for doubt. His friend's idea is really not an option.

"What are you going to do then? Especially since you are getting married soon, right?"

"Yes, of course, that's why I've asked you to come. I would be grateful to have your suggestions. But forget abortion, I can't imagine doing that."

Tshiamwa drinks up the rest of his beer, takes a deep breath and puts down his glass with a somewhat somber gesture. He lifts the bottle and pensively contemplates the level of beer left in it, then he pours the remainder in his glass. The foam flows slightly over the edge. He lifts his glass and he looks at it for a time, like someone who's praying. He then shakes his head, finishes the content of the glass and bangs the glass down on the table.

"What are you doing with that glass now?" Ebamba laughs, after observing his friend's odd ritual. "Just two bottles and you are drunk already?" Ebamba laughs some more in gentle mockery.

Tshiamwa ignores him, he just passes his hand over his face as if he wants to wipe his drunkenness away. He breathes in noisily and he pensively pinches his face, then he stretches out his arms. He rolls up the sleeves of his striped white shirt, glances at his watch, and then looks at his friend Ebamba. "You know that you are one of the friends I cherish and appreciate the most, right? I've seen all you have gone through, from your first years of elementary school till our college years. You are a smart guy and I've always thought that some day you'd be a leader in this country of ours..."

Ebamba cuts him off. "We are not dead yet, pal."

"Right. As you say, we are still around and we can still hope that someday it's going to happen."

"Amen!" Ebamba replies with some laughter in his voice.

"So, as I was saying, I respect you and this is why I will be honest with you. What you just told me really comes as a shock. I wonder what's going to become of you. You have no parents and no steady job to speak of. What is Maguy's mom saying about all this? Does she know already?"

"No, we haven't told her yet. Well, I don't know, since she probably cooked this whole thing up with her daughter, it's quite possible that she's well aware, but to my face she pretends she doesn't know…"

"Well, just tell me one thing: are you in love with Maguy or not?"

"Look, Maguy is not ugly. She's actually a beautiful woman, but I've already chosen the woman for my life and it's Eyenga. And now, with my uncle's help, I'm putting together all the things her family has asked for as her dowry."

"Besides the day of the party, how many times have you actually slept together?"

"Well, it's been more than ten times, I think. I don't even remember exactly. That girl is really as hot as they say Mongala women are."

Tshims smiles a little, looks at his friend. He scratches his head and shakes it slowly. "When I think of the opportunity you had with that job at the bank! Are you really sure you want to pass it up?"

"Pal, I already told you what happened, right?"

"I know, but why are you so much against it, huh?"

"Pal, I already told you, I am never going to consent to something like that, as long as I live. Men with men? Not for me, thanks! You hear me?" Ebamba's tone is rising suddenly. Every time Tshims brings up that story he can't suppress his anger.

Tshims gestures to him to keep his voice down. More and more people are flowing into the bar now. "My friend, what are you shouting for? Look, I really don't see what is so scary about being gay. You are passing by your opportunities for nothing. You are a bright, good-looking guy. It's normal that other men might be attracted to you. I have to tell you that I've always liked you a lot myself."

"What? What are you talking about?" Ebamba jumps up as if he's waking suddenly from slumber. He twists his mouth into an angry frown, trying to come to terms with what his friend has just come out with.

"Pal, just listen..."

"Sorry, alright, go ahead."

"Look, I've wanted to tell you for a long time now, but I've always been afraid of how you were going to take it. Sex with a man is nothing wrong, it's just like sleeping with a woman. It's neither witchcraft nor bestiality. I am neither a fiend nor a beast, you know."

Ebamba's eyes open wide as if they are about to fall out of his skull and his mouth is a big circle too. "What!" he cries out, unable to control himself.

People turn around and stare at them. Ebamba stops talking, and Tshims keeps silent. A few moments tick by. Slowly, people around them resume their business and they go back to talking.

"You see now why I was afraid of telling you?"

"Right. I'm sorry, pal."

"No problem, I'm not blaming you. Just remember this: I am gay too. I sleep with women and I sleep with men, but honestly I prefer men, men like you… I have to tell you, Ebamba, I like you immensely and I can give you all you desire, if you will have me."

Ebamba cries out again. "Hey, now, stop this shit! Are you losing your mind?"

People stare at them again. Ebamba stops, lowers his voice and tries to regain his composure. The bystanders lose interest and look away.

"Don't bring up this again, okay?"

A little shaken, Tshiamwa sits back and to calm down his friend, he whispers. "Okay. I am sorry, pal."

Then he continues anyway. "You see, I was afraid you would take it this way, but you have to understand now that these days most of the people in power in this country are into that. Or they are into kids. So, if you join those circles, I can assure you you'll land a good job within a couple of weeks. That bank manager, you see, I went out with him too. We only did it a couple of times. You shouldn't be scared. It's not witchcraft. It's just a form of the love and carnal desire that all humans experience."

Ebamba says nothing. He just looks at his friend who is trying to talk him into going out with men. Tshiamwa is starting to list all the powerful men he knows that are gay. He gives him the details to prove he's not lying. Ebamba just listens, amazed. Tshiamwa goes on to name all of their college teachers he has dated, then mentions their friends and schoolmates. In spite of his surprise, Ebamba realizes that his friend is telling the truth. A lot of things that didn't make much sense to him at the time suddenly become clear.

Tshiamwa keeps talking, revealing more and more astonishing details that boggle Ebamba's mind. He tells Ebamba about the ways that men have sex, the places where they meet, and the small things they wear or signs they use to recognize each other, like wearing an earring in the left ear or tight-fitting pants that mold to the legs and the butt, drawing their eyebrows with eyeliner or relaxing one's hair, or stroking your hand with a finger when you shake hands, and many other signs…

Tshiamwa tells Ebamba to look discreetly behind him and shows him a politician who's sipping his drink and reading a newspaper in a corner of the bar. When Ebamba shifts his gaze, Tshiamwa whispers that that guy dates men too.

"I know him very well, I've seen him several times in one or other of our usual bars. Don't be surprised though if he pretends not to know me. In fact he's already asked me more than once to go out with him. But I told him no. I even have his number in my phone here."

"And tell me, why did you turn him down? "

"Well, I may be gay, but come on, that doesn't mean I'm willing to date all the gays in Kinshasa. Besides, rumor has it that he's slept with a good number of people in Kinshasa, and some even say he's got AIDS. That's why I don't want to go out with him."

"And who are you dating these days?"

"Well, it's a bit complicated. I was going out with one of the Prime Minister's advisers, but lately we don't get along that well and I'm tired of him. And now I'm thinking of dating people my own age."

He lifts his eyes and looks at Ebamba, one corner of his mouth up in a smile. He touches Ebamba lightly and adds, "Like you."

Ebamba barks out, "Stop that!"

Tshiamwa takes his hand away. He sees very well now that he doesn't stand a chance with his friend.

Ebamba repeats once more that if Tshiamwa values their friendship he's got to stop trying to suggest they might go out together.

It's getting late. The sun is beginning to go down. It is already 5:15 p.m. Having drunk four bottles of Primus, Tshiamwa asks Ebamba if he would like to have a bite to eat. Ebamba nods. They beckon the waitress to the table and order some food. The girl tells them that when you order food, you have to pay right away, it's written on a sign up there.

Tshiamwa pulls a stack of money out from his pocket and starts counting. He hands out a note for the drinks they have had so far. Ebamba thanks him. As he had invited his friend out, he had actually expected to pick up the tab. Tshiamwa waves off his thanks. He has quite a bit of money on him, it hasn't been long since payday.

Ebamba orders malangwa fish, manioc leave pondu, caterpillars, and fufu. Tshiamwa asks for catfish, bitekuteku leaves, plantains and cassava bread.

Right then, they hear the loud crash of two vehicles colliding. People outside start shouting and the patrons of the bar rush out to see what's happening, leaving their bottles and glasses behind. Ebamba and Tshiamwa stand up too and join the commotion outside.

An awful business: a Mercedes 207 minivan has just smashed into a motorbike, beating both the motorbike driver and his lady customer into a pulp. After that, the minivan barreled on, lodging itself into the cement barriers along the roadside.

There are pools of blood all over the pavement.

The motorbike driver and his passenger have died on the spot. Among the passengers of the 207 minivan, quite a few are wounded or have bone fractures. In the blink of an eye, a crowd has formed at the scene. Those with stronger stomachs are rushing to pull the wounded out on their backs so they can be transported to the closest hospitals.

The commotion goes on and on. The soft-hearted are just standing there, crying at the horrible sight of the young driver's and his passenger's bodies, torn to pieces on the road. You couldn't bring yourself to look twice. The motorbike has been flattened, a total wreck. There is a severed arm, intestines overflowing from a body—it is unbearable. Blood runs everywhere, like a river.

While some are crying or trying to help those who are stuck in the vehicle, others have descended on the scene to take advantage of the situation and steal as much as they can. A shameful, wretched sight.

The Red Cross and the police have arrived, ordering people to disperse. The police then proceed to arrest the minivan driver and his conductor, pulling him out of the clutches of the bystanders who had begun to beat him up. Those still around have been pushed aside.

The newspeople of Lingala-Facile, Papa-Molière, Infos-Lingala, CNL, and many other TV stations are rushing over, even those who are never there for ordinary local news, and they are already pulling out their cameras and microphones to interview the witnesses. The amazing thing is that though everyone's giving their account of what they witnessed, there are a million different versions of the event. Everyone tells it their own way and no one version matches the other: one blames the driver of the minivan, another blames the motorbike, another claims it's the fault of the policeman directing traffic, another still blames the Chinese for how they built the road and the government which has let them build it, others blame the neighborhood's witches…

The following day, it rained all morning. Hardly a downpour, just a constant, ceaseless drizzle. People resigned themselves to getting about their business in spite of it.

In the afternoon, the sun came back in full force. It dried out all the streets and people were quickly strained to walk around in the full heat.

At about 5:15 p.m., when the sun was about to set, a fresh breeze had come back—a nice one. The sky had become as rusty as blood and after some time a black cloud covered it, like it was going to rain again, but it didn't linger long—all was swept away by a strong wind. A thin fog set in as the night filled the city.

Ebamba saw the branch of a palm tree pushed into the ground on the corner of the Eyenga's street, as if there were people in mourning somewhere, but Ebamba didn't really think about it. He walked to the gate to Eyenga's compound and he saw then it was open, with people sitting here and there in the yard, their heads down. It then dawned on him that there was indeed a wake happening in the compound. He got to Eyenga's door and just as he was about to knock, someone drew the curtains open and Eyenga came out to kiss him in welcome.

Eyenga brought out two chairs for her and her man, while Ebamba stepped in to greet those inside the house. Only Eyenga's mother and her little sisters were there, watching TV and chatting. Eyenga's mom held out her hand to him and he approached to say hello. She asked him how he was and they made some small talk. With some hesitation, Ebamba asked her who had died and she just sighed, saying that it was a very painful case. She then waved at him to join his fiancée, who would explain everything at length if he wished.

As he was taking leave of them to join Eyenga, Ebamba beckoned to her little sister and asked for some cold water, but the girl told him they didn't have any—there had been a power cut for an entire day and electricity had just come back on. Ebamba nodded, resigned.

Eyenga moved the chair closer to her for Ebamba to take a seat and as soon as he was comfortable, Donate, Eyenga's little sister, the baby of the family, arrived with a pitcher of water and a metal cup. She filled the cup and Ebamba emptied it in one go, then he waved to her to give him some more. As she was pouring, he beckoned to her to stop, drank again, and gave her back the cup, thanking her. Donate smiled, and with a glance to her sister, turned around and went back into the house.

"How... How are you?" Eyenga asked him, to break the ice.

"Hmmph. Fine! But I don't understand, you are mourning someone and you won't even tell me about it. Three days have gone by and I didn't hear a single a word from you. What's the matter?"

"Hey, w-wait, d-don't be angry, eh?"

Eyenga sometimes spoke with a bit of a stutter and apparently that was the case today.

Eyenga was a real beauty. Shiny, smooth dark skin, her neck made lovelier by the two folds her plumpness gave her. Small but curvy, she had all the charms that attract men like bees to honey. On top of that, she was a good girl and even sang in the choir at the Catholic church in her neighborhood.

Her stutter was unique to her. Sometimes it came on, and then suddenly it vanished and she went back to speaking normally. She couldn't say herself what prompted it and in the past she had tried in vain to get rid of it. Those who knew her had gotten used to it and to them it was even pleasing to the ear. People also liked that when she laughed, her dimples came out and she showed her lovely teeth, white as ivory, with a charming little gap between her front teeth that only added to her beauty.

"I-I t-tried to c-call you but the call wouldn't go through... I even thought of passing by your house to-night to see you, but now here you are. You read my mind apparently, s-sweetie!"

She smiled.

"Hmm!" Ebamba smiled back. "So tell me darling, what's going on here? Who died?"

"Ha, honey, something really awful! If you had been around yesterday, you would have seen a mind-boggling sight!"

Eyenga squirmed on her seat.

"The compound was packed with people, the police came, and even the people from the news..."

"What happened then? Who died?"

"The landlord killed the neighbors's kid with witch-craft!"

"With witchcraft?" Ebamba said, stunned. "What do you mean?"

"Ha, it's unbelievable, honey! Kinshasa makambo, as they say. You're always in for some surprise here." Ey-enga's stutter was gone and she continued "It was a little kid who died, named Merdi, just eight years old. No sign of any illness, not even the slightest issue, and then all of sudden at the break of dawn, just like that, the kid is dead.

"And that's why you say that the landlord killed the kid with witchcraft?"

"Oh no, I'm not finished—wait. People didn't blame him just like that, with no good reason. Don't you see that their apartment is wide open and there's no one home? They're all gone... Believe me, Ebamba, that guy really is into witchcraft."

Eyenga told him the whole story. What had happened was, a few days back, that man, the landlord, suddenly demanded that all the tenants who were a couple of months behind on their rent to pay up at once. Eyenga's family paid their debts and was fine. Actually, they had long decided to pay him what he was owed as soon as they could, because in the past the landlord had put them through hell.

One day, soon after they had moved in, they got late on the water bill and the landlord locked the faucet to bar them from using it. He did the same thing with electricity and he even took the outrageous measure of locking the gate after 8 p.m. At 8 p.m. sharp he would close the gate with a big lock and chain, and he wouldn't open it for anyone, grown-up or child. If you couldn't climb over the tall wall, it was your problem. If there was an interruption in the water service, he would lock the toilets, so the tenants wouldn't soil them. Just like him to do something like that. One day he'd even scooped up a bucketful of excrement and thrown it all right in front of his tenants's door, because he'd gotten into his head that they and their kids were filling up his toilets beyond what he thought reasonable. That incident had caused a big uproar in the compound.

Yesterday's events had been awful: the landlord had again told the tenants they must pay their rent as soon as possible because he was in a hurry to pay his children's school fees. This time he didn't stop there. He threatened that if they wouldn't be quick to pay up, he'd take their kids. He had been very clear. He'd publicly said that if they didn't give him what he was owed their kids would die.

The tenants had taken it as a gross joke, although the way he had said it would send chills down your spine. He swore it in front of them all and he even uttered a few magical spells right there.

Scared, Eyenga's family hastened to pay that month's rent on time. The other tenants didn't have the money handy and had promised the landlord they would pay within a couple of days, but he had adamantly refused the offer and added that they would come to regret it.

That night, there had been no peace in the compound. Cats howled all night long. You could hear them roam and run on the roof. They howled like small children, exactly like that. And when they finally stopped, it had been the dogs's turn to bark furiously and yelp. As soon as they stopped, there had been an eerie silence in the middle of the night and then, right at that moment, the neighbors's kid had cried out loudly and passed out. The child was even foaming at the mouth.

That night, around 4 a.m., the whole family rushed to the small clinic nearby, but it was already too late. The kid's heart had stopped beating along the way and there was nothing the doctors could do. They couldn't even tell what had caused the child to die so quickly. There had been no signs of any kind of illness or pain.

The death had terrified and pained everyone in the neighborhood. People started mourning at the crack of dawn and a crowd had poured in at the clinic.

When they'd come back from the hospital, the compound was in complete havoc. Not at all surprisingly, in spite of the din, the landlord's door remained closed, as if he hadn't heard anything. Seeing his reaction, the neighbors soon realized that the witch who'd stopped their kid's heart right in its prime was indeed not very far away.

In fact, after hearing the whole story, including the landlord's threats and declarations, they had quickly concluded it was him that had killed the child, just as he had promised!

After that, a sizable crowd, of youngsters especially, had marched to the landlord's door and started to bang on it, and even to throw stones. Armed with sticks, they'd broken bottles and burned tires, shouting that they'd kill him as soon as laid hands on him. To show him they meant business, they'd started to shake the door to force it open, but they hadn't succeeded because the door was made of solid iron. So they had smashed all the window panes and even the glass squares in the door.

The huge havoc soon drew in the police and even the mayor rushed to the compound, with a crowd of journalists on his heels. As soon as the mayor stepped into the yard, the police fired a few shots in the air to disperse the crowd and cool down the hotheads. The mayor spent some time with Merdi's family, who explained how the events leading up to Merdi's death had unfolded. He offered soothing words and assured them that he would take care of everything concerning the child's burial.

The mayor then evacuated the landlord and all of his family, all crammed in one of the police cars, saying they would be taken to the police station to tell their side of the story, and that a police statement drawn up.

The police had done their best to protect them from the menacing crowd, but the landlord and his family had nevertheless been shaken up. They had sticks thrown at them, and bottles and stones too. In fact, one of his daughters had even been wounded on the head.

The agents had once again fired a few shots in the air to keep the people off of them. You could really tell that if they hadn't been there, with the mayor in tow, the landlord and his family would have been taken care of by the crowd. They would have certainly burned them with gasoline and tires.

Ebamba had followed the story open mouthed with astonishment. He had listened to Eyenga's tale with panic, his throat closed with anguish. He even found it hard to swallow. And he couldn't help feeling furious at the unbearable things that the tenants had had to put up with.

"And now what, are they still at the police station?"

"Sure, they are still there." Eyenga said that they were probably still being held there because the police feared that if they were allowed back into their home, the neighbors would seize them and beat them to death.

Some people had followed them to the police station anyhow, insulting them and shouting "Witch! witch!" as loud as they could...

When night came, Ebamba and Eyenga were still deep in conversation. They had left her compound and had walked to a bar across the street to continue with their lovers's talk with greater privacy. It was an open air bar—no lights, no music, just a space enclosed by flower bushes and lidame trees, so thick that the mayor had told the owners over and over again to prune them because it made the street look messy, like a tree sprawling right across the road. ""Enlevez-moi cette broussaille!" he exclaimed in his most official French, every time he walked around, surrounded by military.

One day he had actually sent over people to cut the "weeds," as he called them, at a local bar called As de Pic, while the bar owner glared at them. They had even exchanged insults. Bystanders looked on with astonishment, but the mayor didn't have the owner arrested. He just told his people to keep cutting the vegetation, and the place was now bare. In the following days, usual customers had avoided the As de Pic, because many of them, men and women alike, went there with their partners because the vegetation had made the place discreet. As you didn't have to worry you would be easily spotted there, the bar was widely known as Kuzu, which means "hiding."

Eyenga and Ebamba were sitting together at a very discreet bar of that kind. Not many customers were around at that time. They ordered two sodas and the waitress immediately brought over two big bottles of Vitalo and a couple of glasses.

The night was not pitch dark—the full moon was out and its brightness filled the whole sky.

Just as he was about to say something, Ebamba's phone rang loudly. Ebamba slipped his hand in his pocket and drew out his phone. He looked at the name flashing on the screen and turned down the call. Eyenga was surprised. "Why didn't you take the call?"

"It's just problems." Ebamba put back the phone in his pocket and told Eyenga, "Just a friend of mine. You know him too, Dodi Mazita. I owe him a little money. I told him to be patient, I'm going to call him when I have the money to pay him back. Now he's harassing me like it's some big problem. A big deal over nothing."

"Come on, how can you say something like that, Ebamba? You're dead wrong, you know. You owe him, you have to pay him back, so he has every right to keep calling you, doesn't he? If he hadn't lent you the money you needed, you would have been in a bad spot, right? And besides, you don't even know if he's calling you about that. What if he's calling you for a totally different reason, huh? Maybe he's calling you to tell you about some job or a small deal that'll make you some money!"

"What? No! You don't know Dodi then! Dodi calling me over a job or business? Just as likely as seeing angels walk the earth, you know! Let's just change the subject, okay?"

"No, don't say that! I know you don't like people to give you advice and you won't listen anyway… And besides, let me tell you, don't you think I'm taking your word for it just like that. How am I to know for sure it was really your *male* friend Dodi!" Saying this, Eyenga looked very angry. Pointing a finger at him she added, "Look, Ebamba, I've heard rumors about you and people have told me what you are doing. People who've seen you with a woman at this place or that."

Ebamba sat back, startled, and gave her an angry look. "What the hell do you mean?"

"Don't pretend you don't know what I'm talking about! Look, I'm warning you, this will be the first and last time I'm telling you before I catch you at it!"

"Well, Eyenga, I didn't know you believed rumors!"

"Ah, f-forget it! As they say, water doesn't move by itself. If they talk about it, there must be a reason."

"Oh, Eyenga!"

Eyenga was furious. All of her pleasure had vanished. She crossed her arms and looked away. Tender-hearted as she was, tears started flowing down her cheeks. Refusing to look at Ebamba, she started sniffling. Ebamba called her name once again, sadly, with a tone of supplication, but she wouldn't look at him or break her angry pose.

Ebamba reached out to comfort her with his touch. With tender persistence, he managed to draw her close. He put his arm over her shoulders and tried his best to comfort her. Eyenga rested her head on his shoulder.

Very tenderly, Ebamba dried her tears and smoothed her hair, then handed her a drink. Eyenga took a sip, lifted her eyes, and asked him to buy her a bottle of cold water to drink.

Ebamba asked the waiter to fetch him a big bottle of chilled water. Once the water was served, Eyenga took a sip, and then Ebamba took one in turn. Eyenga laid her head back on her man's shoulder, closed her eyes and fell into a peaceful doze.

Very softly, Ebamba started humming a song by Koffi Olomide, the great Mopao, into Eyenga's ear, which goes:

Yo ozali se wa ngai,
You are mine alone

Nazali se wa yo…
I am yours…

Then they both sang the duet:

Nakofuta na ngai mbongo té
No money have I to pay

Oza ya ofele
Your love is for free

Nakokima pe mbangu té
I don't have to chase you

Oza pene na ngai
You're right by my side

Nakoluka pe zuzi té
I don't have to seek a judge

Dossier eza na yango vide
I am not guilty of any crime

Yo oza kumida oyo naboya kokabola
You are the food I refuse to share

Yo oza nourriture oyo esalema se po na ngai
You are the delicious food prepared for me alone

Ata ami intime asengi, akozwa té
Even if my best friend asked for some, I would refuse

Ata asilisi baverset nyonso ya bible, akolala nzala
Even if he quoted every verse in the Bible, he'd go to
bed hungry

Ata atangisi pinzoli tii ekokauka
Even if he should shed every tear he had

Soki ozalaki ata etabe, Ebamba je t'assure
If you were a banana, Ebamba, I can assure you

Nakobanga na ngai té kobotola yo na maboko ya mokomboso
I wouldn't be afraid to wrestle you even from the
gorilla's hands

Plutôt qu'un jour naya kozanga yo, nandimi liwa
I would rather die than ever lose you

Naza argile…
I am clay…

Yo sculpteur maitre de l'œuvre!
And you are the artist shaping me!

Forme nyonso okopesa…
Any shape you choose to give me…

N*gai nakondima!*
I will accept!

Ata nazocadrer té na valeur na ngai artistique
Even if I don't meet my artistic value

Disproportion pe eza reconnue comme valeur artistique
Even disproportion can be recognized as artistic value

Epai ya baplasticien
Among artists

Simba simba ngai gueye Eyenga nazwa forme
Eyenga, don't stop shaping me with your touch

Yo moko obanda baesquisse,
You are the artist who sketched me into being

Kotika te moto mosusu aya koachever œuvre na yo
Don't let anyone come in and take over your work

De peur que œuvre eperdre pureté na yango
Your work would certainly lose its purity

Silisa ngai yo moko
Give me your finishing touch

Matricule zero zero nazalaki
Even if I am worth nothing

Naboyi batindika ngai ata un milimetre ya pamba
I refuse to be pushed aside even a millimeter

Naboyi kodemarrer na horoscope
I refuse to bow to chance

Fungola na maboko na yo
The key is in your hands

Retraite de priere na ngai
You are my prayer retreat

Nzambe asala ngai faveur
The Lord has given me a gift

Un tiens vaut mieux que deux tu l'auras
Fools say a bird in the hand is worth two in the bush

Bolingo na yo ekotisa ngai nzala na miso
Your love has made me addicted to the sight of you

Ata pe mabe yango eza
Even if something bad comes to pass

Yo signer presence
Please be there for me

Nasi nalatisa yo kazaka ya raison
You are my source of truth

Okomisa ngai baba
You have left me speechless

Maloba nyoso omema
You have taken all words away

Otikela ngai se je t'aime
The only words you've left me with are, *I love you*

Nazali feuille vierge…
I am a blank sheet of paper

Yo stylo lipasa na ngai!
And you are my everlasting pen!

Encre nyonso okokomela…
Regardless of the ink you'll use to write…

Ngai nakondima!
I will accept it!

Aveugle kutu abetaka canne po amona nzela
The blind man taps around with his stick to make his way

Ebamba okomisa ngai aveugle, canne omema
Ebamba you have me blind, you have taken away my stick

Natikala se na yo
You are my only guide now

Eyenga bolingo napesa na yo eleki ata mosolo
Eyenga, the love I have for you is more precious than gold

Ata ba-utiliser bafonds ya fmi po bacorrompre ngai
Even if they offered me all of the IMF's money to bribe me away from you

Nakondima na ngai kobengama mpiakeur
I will rather be called the poorest of the poor

Richesse na ngai se yo Eyenga Kitoko
You are my wealth, beautiful Eyenga

Soki babengi bariche tout ya mokili
If they asked all the millionaires in the world

Batié mituka
To give up their awesome cars

Ata babakisi baavion ya Emirates Airways po natika yo
And they tossed all of Emirates Airways's planes into
the deal for me to give you up

Nakondima na ngai obengama piéton nazala se na yo
Let them call me a pedestrian forever rather than
losing you

Totambola très collés très serrés
Hold me close, so close

Eyenga ata na ligne 11
Eyenga, even if we only have our feet to get us
through life's journey

Cheval na ngai lover ngai
You'll be my horse, love me

Mema ngai na mokongo
Carry me on your back

Beta ngai kigi kigi
Gallop away

Eyenga beta ngai kigi kigi
Eyenga, gallop away

Linga ngai bolingo linga ngai kigi kigi
Tie me to you, my love, tie me to you and gallop away

Ebamba bolingo na yo vraiment soki ezalaki elamba ya kolata
Ebamba, my love, if you were a garment

Nakondima na ngai kotingama na piece moko tout le reste de la vie
I would choose to wear just one garment for the rest of my life

Ata kutu John Galliano acréer bapiece prototype
Even if John Galliano showered me with his creations

Nakotingama na ngai na polo se moko Ebamba lokola Lucky Luke
I will only wear that one T-shirt, Ebamba, like Lucky Luke

Ebamba mema ngai mema ngai na mokongo
Ebamba, carry me, carry me on your back

Love ngai kigi kigi
My love, gallop away

Enfant de Mbandaka lover ngai kigi kigi
Child of Mbandaka, love me, gallop away

Mema ngai na mokongo mema ngai
Carry me on your back, carry me

Kokoma bolingo nayebi te nayebi se kolover yo…
I don't know how to write the word love, I only know how to love you…

While they were singing, some were drinking in the darkness of the bar. Others were kissing greedily.

The wind that carries the rain was blowing stronger and some drops started falling suddenly. People started to scatter. After a quick last kiss, Eyenga dashed off, back to her house. Ebamba stopped a moto-taxi and made his way home too. It was really late…

"Hey, stop ignoring me! I'm talking to you!" Maguy insisted, trying to get Ebamba to stop stalling and finally answer her. "I'm asking you again. Where were you last night?"

Ebamba grimaced as if he wanted to laugh it off, but Maguy froze him in his tracks. "Don't laugh, there's nothing funny about it."

"Come on…" Ebamba couldn't find anything to say. He gave Maguy a confused look as if he didn't understand what she was getting at, and pursued, "Where do you think I was? I went out to see my uncle and the rain caught me while I was at his house."

"And you couldn't answer when I called you? And you even turned off your phone? You think I'm a fool, huh?" Maguy's tone was escalating. She was really furious.

"The battery was low and the phone turned itself off right when you called me. And there was a power outage there!"

Maguy let out a sound of astonishment, then clapped her hands and cracked her knuckles.

Ebamba was simply lying, of course. He was with Eyenga yesterday, when Maguy had called, and that's why he hadn't taken the call. Women have a sort of built-in sixth sense—when their men are lying, they invariably pick it up.

Maguy found it really hard to believe Ebamba's story, but since he kept insisting that he was telling the truth, she didn't pursue it any further. She backed off and just changed the subject.

The sun was not shining that bright. You would think it was ashamed to show itself to the world. It had been hiding behind the clouds since the morning. On the street, they were joking that the angel in charge was in a good mood today. And usually, when the sun is mercilessly scorching the earth, they say that the angel on duty must be a new hire.

It was Thursday morning—10:12 a.m. Ebamba and Maguy were lounging in Ebamba's apartment, having breakfast and making small talk. Every now and then, they exchanged some kiss or caress.

Ebamba was just wearing shorts—no shirt on. By his side, Maguy had a wrap on, and a silky skimpy top which definitely didn't hide her curves. She wasn't wearing a bra.

They were lounging on his bed and they had put a stool in front of it where they had placed a tray with all the delicacies of their breakfast: bread, sugar, a dish of margarine, bags of milk, tea…

While they were chatting and eating, Ebamba's ringtone suddenly came on very loudly. The phone was charging on the other side of the room, so Maguy got up to bring it over to Ebamba. She unplugged it from the outlet, but as the mobile kept relentlessly ringing, she looked down at the screen. The number was showing but not the name of the caller. Without thinking much of it, she just handed the phone to Ebamba.

Ebamba looked at the number and turned down the incoming call. Surprised, Maguy asked him why he hadn't taken it. Just as he was about to reply, the tune started again. He picked up the phone and when he saw it was the same number calling, he turned it down again and switched it off.

Maguy was truly amazed. You could read the astonishment on her face. "Who was it?" she asked.

"Just problems, honey. These days I have stopped taking calls when I don't recognize the number."

Ebamba was working up a sweat, and Maguy couldn't hide her surprise. The incident was bothering her, and it was clear to her that her man was hiding something, but she ended up shrugging it off. *It doesn't really matter*, she told herself. *He's mine now. All the others will get tired at some point, but I certainly won't let him slip away*. But all she said was, "Fine."

She puffed her cheeks a bit, as if to say there was no problem at all, sitting down again next to Ebamba on his bed. They resumed their chat, picking up a bit of food every now and then and touching each other often.

A few minutes later, with no warning knock, the door opened and the curtain was pulled aside to reveal an unexpected visitor: Eyenga herself!

The two lovers squirmed, suddenly panicking. Ebamba sat up, quickly drawing away from Maguy. Maguy herself instinctively had jumped up in alarm, but when she saw who it was, she relaxed. She remained quite calm, although she was rather surprised at the way Ebamba had quickly put some distance between them.

Eyenga had rushed in without knocking and she had surprised them in a guilty position: they had been kissing and Maguy's hand was lingering on Ebamba's shoulder.

A thunderbolt—a thunderbolt in clear skies, as Mpongo Love sings, struck through Eyenga's heart. She didn't know what to do. Stunned, she just stood here, motionless, like someone who has been electrocuted. She was speechless. Her eyes were open wide like they were popping out of her skull. She rubbed them with her hand as if she wanted to wake up from a nightmare. What she was seeing couldn't possibly be real! That couldn't be her man doing that, it couldn't be happening to her! And yet…

The three of them remained silent for a few moments, frozen in their spots. No one said a word. They stared at each other as if they were dead, as if it were raining and lightning had struck them.

"W-what i-is g-going on here?" Eyenga exclaimed. She was so upset that she was stuttering uncontrollably. She couldn't get out her words, her voice was strangled in her throat with the grief, jealousy, and anguish she felt. The tears were already filling up her eyes and were just about to flow.

Eyenga raised her hands to her head. "I-I am a-asking you, Ebamba. W-what is this?" Eyenga asked again, at the top of her lungs. Ebamba remained silent, not knowing what to say. He was deeply ashamed. He lowered his eyes and just shook his head.

When Maguy realized that Ebamba was unable to react, she hastened to speak. "Honey, why on earth are you embarrassed?" With a disdainful look at Eyenga, Maguy went on. "Who's this woman who barges in on us like that? You—what are you looking for here, huh? You come in without knocking, no respect for people's home? What is this, the street? Who do you think you are, huh?"

This enraged Eyenga even more. "What are you saying, huh, you whore? Don't you remember me? How dare you call my man honey right in front of me? What is this, huh?"

"Be careful, you be careful!" Annoyed, Maguy stood up and knotted her wrap more tightly."

"Be careful, you! Who are you calling a whore, huh? Me?" Pointing at herself, she shouted, "Is it me you are calling a whore? Do you know me?"

"Don't take that tone with me, I am not your friend! I have seen you around this compound and I don't care that you are the owner's daughter! Stay away from my man!"

The argument was escalating into a real fight. The two women were an centimeter away from each other, about to come to blows. As things were spiraling out of control, Ebamba stood up and, bare chested as he was, rushed to separate the two women, pushing them away from each other, but the women wouldn't stop arguing furiously, hurling all sorts of insults at each other.

"Honey, tell your whore to get out of my house! Tell her!" Eyenga shouted at Ebamba.

Ebamba turned towards Maguy as if to calm her down and ask her to step out for a moment, but Maguy guessed what he was about to say and that fueled her anger even more, so she shouted at Ebamba, "What are you doing, huh? She's leaving, not me! Tell that bitch to get out of here, or I'll make you regret it!"

Ebamba just stood there, looking dumb. He didn't know what to do, so he remained rooted to the spot like a fool, while the two women kept insulting each other at the top of their voices.

The yard was quickly filling with idle onlookers who came to enjoy the show. Women, men, young people, grown-ups, and kids were crowding into Maguy's compound, shoving each other to get in front of Ebamba's door. Everyone was eager to see what was going on inside, fighting and pushing each other aside to get a better look at the commotion.

Before long, a woman rushed to the scene, holding one of those big sticks used to make fufu. It was the landlady, Mama Mongala, who demanded that they let her through, so she could get in. Since everyone knew her, they did as they were told without a word of protest.

Mama Mongala stepped in. "What's going on in here?" She shouted angrily with her intimidating voice, looking at her daughter and Ebamba.

Maguy immediately pointed an accusing finger at Eyenga. "It's that trashy woman, showing up from God knows where! She had the nerve to shout at my man to get me out of here!"

Needless to say, Mama Mongala already knew Eyenga, and she hardly had to be told what was going on, but she pretended to be shocked and outraged at what her daughter was saying. Eyenga tried to talk but the landlady didn't let her get in a word. Ebamba tried to say something too, but the landlady silenced him. Mama Mongala ordered Eyenga to get out of the house unless she wanted things to end badly. "You, get out of my house right now!"

Eyenga was stunned by her words but stood her ground. "Why would I get out, huh? You may be the owner of this compound, but this is my man's apartment—he pays the rent here. I'm not going to leave unless he asks me to."

"He pays the rent? With what money, huh?" Mama Mongala laughed at Eyenga with a look of contempt. "That's right, ask him! Who does he pay the rent to?"

Eyenga was very surprised to hear those words. She looked at Ebamba but he couldn't withstand her gaze for long. For the past few months, since he had started dating the landlady's daughter, Ebamba had in fact no longer been paying his rent. Even his deposit had long run out, but he had never told Eyenga.

Astonished and humiliated, Eyenga realized there was a lot she didn't know and that since so much had been hidden from her, it was more than likely that her man was indeed dating the other woman.

Eyenga felt as if all the blood had been drained from her. Her left hand on her hip, she raised her other hand to her lips and bit down hard on her ring finger. It crossed her mind that quite a few acquaintances had told her they had seen her man around town with another woman, in very funny places and behaving strangely, but she had never been told the woman's name and she had always been skeptical.

Now she couldn't say anything. A brief silence filled the room, till the landlady spoke again. "Come on, get out! Get *out*! I don't want problems in my house! Get out, you hear?"

Eyenga stood there like a statue, out of words. Ebamba didn't know what to say either, right then.

Tears were streaming down Eyenga's cheeks. Her arms hanging at her hips, she looked at Ebamba.

The landlady wouldn't stop. "Hey you, are you deaf or what? I told you to get out! Out!" Mama Mongala shouted again at the top of her voice, adding, "In case you didn't know, I'll tell you, your thing with this man here is long finished! He's my daughter's man now, and besides they are about to give me my first grandchild. You see my daughter there, Maguy? She's already big with the kid Ebamba has put in her belly."

The landlady had spoken in those rough terms because she was aiming to shock Eyenga as much as she could. The words had rekindled Eyenga's suffering, especially when she heard that the landlady's daughter was expecting Ebamba's child. Eyenga had no words left in her. A flood of tears fell from her eyes and she no longer bothered to dry them.

She looked once more at Ebamba and with deep grief she whispered, "E-Ebamba! T-thank you!"

Without adding anything, she let out a deep sigh and made for the door.

Bakaké ezanga mvula
The thunder without rain

Ebeti na motema na ngai
Has struck my heart

Motema mobebi
My heart is broken

Nakoki té ooooh
I can't stand the pain

Bolingo ngai nakaba mingi
All the love I gave

Lelo bafuti ngai lifuta ya punda eeeeh
And today I get ingratitude in return

Motema ya mwana na moto nzoka esuwaka boye.
My heart is bitten by grief

Ngai nakei ehhhh
I'm leaving

Solo nakei komipemisa na ngai
I am leaving to seek shelter

Motema mwa ngai mokei na nkele,
My heart has gone into the land of bitterness

Motema mwa ngai…
My heart…

Mabanzo ma ngai makei na nkele
My thoughts have gone into the land of bitterness

Mabanzo ma ngai…
My thoughts…

Motema mwa ngai mokei na nkele
My heart has gone into the land of bitterness

Motema mwa ngai…
My heart…

Mabanzo ma ngai makei na nkele
My thoughts have gone into the land of bitterness

Mabanzo ma ngai…
My thoughts…

Bakoyebisa ngai balobi:
Just as they have told me:

Bolingo ezali na suka tè
Love is not worth the effort

Natika eehh
I give up

Nalembi koyoka ya basango ya mama ahhh
I am tired of hearing news of my lover

Na mokili baloba balemba dis ehhh
On this Earth they have talked and talked until they
were breathless

Bakomata lelo, lobi bakokita
In life you can rise today and fall tomorrow

Natika eeeh
And I give up

Nalembi koyoka ya basango ya mama ahhh
I am tired of hearing news of my lover

It was as noisy as the market but there was no one around. On top of the human noise, you could hear cats letting out piercing shrieks and dogs barking. The wind carrying the rain was blowing but the air was as hot as if someone was heating it up. It was pitch dark everywhere. You couldn't see anyone, you could just hear the noise.

Right at that moment I heard Eyenga's voice in the distance, crying in the darkness. She was shouting my name with sorrow. It terrified me. I moved closer to get a look, but I couldn't see anything. The more I advanced, the more the voice distanced.

Eyenga was crying, her voice full of sorrow and sadness, but I couldn't see her anywhere, not even her shadow. She cried out my name three times, and I replied to ask her where she was, so I could see her, but she kept silent.

The clouds were as black as coal. I saw a flock of bats, a swarm of termites flying about, then a flock of eagles, of owls, and then of birds of all kinds. They were flying here and there, disorderly, and suddenly they rushed towards me as if they meant to catch me… Right then, thunder rang out in the sky, the wind had become strong. A great, terrifying flock of birds approached at high speed and they touched down on the ground near me…

"Oh God!"

Because he was terrified by the dream, Maguy held Ebamba in her arms. "Oh God, what an awful nightmare you must have had, darling!"

Ebamba didn't reply. His heart was beating madly and he was sweating. They were sitting in his bed, still quite upset by Ebamba's scream when he had been jolted out of sleep by the nightmare.

Ebamba described his nightmare to Maguy from start to finish, but he kept some details to himself, because they were even more terrifying. They remained motionless for a while. Ebamba was totally disconcerted by the dream he'd had. Questions were whirling around in his mind. What could the dream mean?

That night, there had been a power outage and they'd gone to bed in complete darkness. Ebamba stood up and lit a candle he placed in a plate filled with water.

Thirty minutes had gone by since Ebamba had woken up from his nightmare. It was 3:52 a.m. It was still very dark outside, and at such an hour sleepiness is overwhelming. Although he was still shaken, when Maguy slipped back into slumber Ebamba couldn't help being swept towards the treacherous trap one cannot avoid at that time of night and dozed off as well.

A pack of terrifying black hounds was furiously chasing Ebamba. He couldn't run very well. He felt as if his legs were tied together with ropes. He tried to run, but he kept falling, and the hounds were catching up with him. They were so fast they were already closing in. Suddenly, Ebamba saw a big hole right in front of him. He couldn't jump over it in any way. His heart thumped to a stop and he froze in his tracks. Looking over his shoulder, he saw the pack of hounds catching up… The hounds pounced on Ebamba, about to sink their teeth into him… At that moment, Ebamba screamed and jumped out of his sleep.

Maguy woke up startled. For the second time that night, Ebamba was shaken out of sleep. She was again filled with fear and asked Ebamba what the matter was. He told her the story of his second nightmare and Maguy was once more very upset.

When the morning came, the rough night they'd had kept them in bed for longer than usual. It was already past seven when they suddenly woke up…

Ebamba couldn't find the courage to go out. The previous night's nightmares made him feel feverish... From the moment he woke up, he started calling Eyenga's number, but the call wouldn't go through and that did nothing to calm his anguish. He wanted to go out and see his girlfriend Eyenga to make sure she was doing well, to tell her about his nightmare, to ask for forgiveness and start over…

Vany, Maguy's little sister, brought him the aspirin he'd sent her to buy. He took two and gulped them down with the help of some cool water.

Maguy had gone out to sell what her mother had given her at the market, with the intention to stop along the way and buy a small amount of some food or other that Ebamba especially liked, so she could prepare a good meal for him.

Vany kept him company for a while, then left because she had to prepare for school. She attended afternoon classes. Ebamba was left all alone with a whirlwind of bothersome thoughts. He was haunted by the nightmares and the thought of all that had happened the previous day between him and Eyenga.

I'm going to see her! Ebamba told himself. *That nightmare doesn't mean anything good. Eyenga is the woman I had promised to marry, the woman my family knows. What I'm doing is so foolish. It is as if they slipped me a potion. No, I've gone too far… I have crossed the line! Eyenga is my woman. I have to go and see her. I'm going to ask her to forgive me. I know she loves me very much, just as I love her, I know she's going to forgive me!*

Ebamba told himself his decision to go to Eyenga's was firm. He got up and pulled the door closed to change into clean clothes. He looked at himself in the mirror, combed his hair neatly, put on a little cologne and sat back down on his bed to put on his shoes.

Right as he was bending over to pull his shoes out from under the bed, he heard his phone ring. Someone was calling him. He stopped looking for his shoes, stood up, and crossed the room to get his phone from the stool he had left it on. The screen was showing a number but no name. Ebamba hesitated for a second but finally decided to take the call. He slowly raised the phone to his ear and remained silent. He was waiting for the caller to speak first.

"How are you, son? Are you okay?"

"Yes, I'm well, uncle. And you?" Ebamba had immediately recognised the voice of his Uncle Engulu. He was glad to hear from him because it had been a few days since the last time they had seen each other. Ebamba was happy to talk to him…

After a few moments's talk, Ebamba yelled, "No!" and threw down the phone. He fell to the floor, and, holding his arms over his head, he started crying.

The neighbors in the big house and the other tenants heard his cries and rushed to see what had happened to him. Mama Mongala entered, and seeing him on the floor she asked him what was the matter. Helping Ebamba up, she led him to the bed and sat down next to him. Ebamba told her the news his uncle had just given him.

Uncle Engulu had called Ebamba to share the sad news that his Uncle Ebende had died yesterday in the neighborhood called Mpila, in the Congo on the other side of the river.

The news of his death shattered Ebamba. It hit him hard because it was like losing a father. In fact, Uncle Ebende had raised him since he was a small child and he had taken care of everything: his studies, his clothes, his health problems, and everything else. And it was for that very reason that Ebamba was eagerly awaiting his return to resume the negotiations with Eyenga's family and to start buying some of the items they needed for Eyenga's dowry.

Uncle Ebende was a trader and he dealt in many kinds of goods. He sold whatever was in demand at this or that time. Sometimes he sold gasoline, sometimes palm oil, sometimes fish or venison, or clothes and shoes. This time, before death carried him away, he'd traveled to Abidjan to get some new clothes for his business and had made his way to the Congo on the other side of the river before planning to cross over to Kinshasa.

Death surprised him in his house when one of the Brazzaville army's ammunition depots had blown up, and the fire of the explosion had resulted in casualties and damages. Several houses, churches, and clinics had burned down nearby, and there'd been many wounded.

Mama Mongala was sad to hear the news but she did her best to comfort Ebamba and to stop his tears, as he had started crying even harder after he finished telling the story and explaining how important the man who'd just died was to him.

The body of the deceased, Uncle Ebende, was to cross back the river that day around 3 p.m., which was why uncle Engulu had called Ebamba to prepare, so they could go together, along with the other members of the family, to the port downtown, behind the US embassy, where they had opened the new port to cross the river between Kinshasa and Brazzaville.

At first, Ebamba was angry that he had received the news at the last minute even though the news had reached Kinshasa the previous day. Uncle Engulu told him he'd only received the news in the evening and that he'd tried to call Ebamba right away, but his phone seemed disconnected.

Ebamba felt as if his life had stopped. He couldn't stop crying. Mama Mongala tried to comfort him, along with the other neighbors, but to no avail.

Maguy came back a little earlier than usual that day, as her mother had asked someone to call her to pass on the sad news of Ebamba's uncle. She decided to give up on the other errands she had planned to do after the market, like having her hair braided and a few other small things. After canceling everything, she rushed back home and she found Ebamba in her mother's arms, crying like a small child with swollen eyes, his face wet with tears. She was saddened to see him in that state and she was brought to tears too.

Mama Mongala told Maguy all that Ebamba had told her and explained the importance of the deceased to him. Maguy sat on the other side of the bed and started to dry Ebamba's tears.

"This is really awful, Mom! And we didn't sleep all night, Ebamba had one nightmare after the other and he was shaken out of sleep again and again…"

Maguy embarked on the story of what happened the previous night to show her mom that it was as if something dark had happened that night and that the nightmares were a sign for Ebamba. As Maguy was telling everything to her mother, Ebamba shuddered and added more details from the nightmares he'd had during the night.

Ebamba's phone rang again: this time it was one of Ebamba's aunts living in Brazzaville, asking if Ebamba had received the news of his uncle's death. He talked for some time with her and she explained the circumstances of his death and how they had found the body. After hearing all the details from his aunt, he couldn't hold back the tears.

But surprises just weren't over for him.

At that very moment, a small crowd erupted into the compound and angrily rushed into Ebamba's apartment. It was three strong young men, accompanied by a man and a woman.

"Where is the guy called Ebamba?"

The question was asked with some brutality, as soon as they set foot in the yard, before they spotted Ebamba.

When they laid eyes on him, the older man spoke up. "Ebamba, what have you done to our child?"

Startled, Ebamba sat back and looked at them with incomprehension, since he had never seen them.

"What? What child are you talking about?"

"I see you are pretending you don't know..."

"But, sir..."

"Look, we haven't come here to waste time on useless chatter..." Angrily, the man pointed his finger at Ebamba and told him, "Know this—you are going to pay for shedding our child's blood. It's on your hands!"

A terrifying thunderbolt struck Ebamba's heart. He stood up, stopped crying. and started feverishly questioning himself what this was all about. Since the man had started talking, Ebamba hadn't been able to understand who the man was talking about, because he hadn't said who his child was.

"What child are you talking about, sir?" he asked once more, his heart in anguish, refusing to hear and to believe what they were about to say, since it was in fact what he feared.

They all replied in a single shout, "Eyenga!"

"What?"

As soon as he heard the answer, Ebamba fell to the ground like a corpse.

As a matter of fact, that morning they had found Eyenga's lifeless body hanging with a rope around her neck from an avocado tree behind her house. On the ground they found a piece of paper with a pencil right beside it. On the paper, she had written, "Thank you, Ebamba."

They tried to shake Ebamba back to life with every means they could think of, but their efforts were useless. They rushed him to the nearest clinic, but there too, they couldn't do anything for him.

Richard Ali A Mutu was born in Mbandaka, Democratic Republic of the Congo, in 1988. He won the Mark Twain Award in 2009, and published his first novel, *Tabu's Nightmares*, written in French, in 2011. His novel *Ebamba: Kinshasa Makambo*, translated into English as *Mr. Fix-It*, was published in Lingala in 2014. Ali A Mutu was selected as the only writer working primarily in an indigenous African language for the Africa39 anthology, which showcased the continent's most talented writers under the age of forty, including Chimamanda Ngozi Adichie and Ingoni A. Barrett. He works as a lawyer and writer, and hosts a weekly television program about Congolese literature.

Bienvenu Sene Mongaba is a Congolese writer, translator, and publisher. He directs Éditions Mabiki, which champions Congolese languages. He has written three books of fiction in Lingala and several in French. He splits his time between Kinshasa and Belgium.

An avid reader and passionate linguist with a keen academic interest in African literature, **Sara Sene** is a translator working with Italian, English, French, Spanish, and Lingala.

CPSIA information can be obtained
at www.ICGtesting.com
Printed in the USA
LVOW12s1440210717
542097LV00005B/8/P